YAMALY, THE SEA-DINO

Amina Harrison

YAMALY, THE SEA-DINO

CHAPTER ONE

Let's go outside, to the beach and see if we can see *it,*" a young, island child of twelve years of age, by the name of Jearl Allan is saying to her other two best friends, who live on the island of the Bahamas with her; Onandi and Sandie Bello. The three island children have been the best friends, for as long as all three can remember. As the three island children, are just sitting around a stretch of beach, along a tiny town located in the Bahamas Island, as they wait to go and see a make-believe sea-dino known as the *Yamaly*.

Before the three island children were born, there had been stories and tales, which was always about a strange, yet almost fairy-tale sea creature, which can be seen, during a night of a full moon. Since those days, any other peoples of the Bahamas Island, has not really seen the so-called sea creature. Only one man, who has actually seen the by now known as the *Yamaly the sea-dino*, has seen the sea creature.

"We can wait until the sun sets, then maybe we can see it," says Sandie Bello, who has heard some other fairy tales about the sea creature. Sandi did not want to tell her other best friend Jearl Allan, at times Sandie would be afraid if the *make-believe*, sea creature would ever walk upon the shores of the beach, close to their near, small island, where all three of the island children live.

"We could, but our parents maybe worried," says the other island child Onandie Bello, who although he believes the sea creature exists, mostly because Onandie has been told some of the fairy tales, by his uncle

Joel Ato; one of Onandi and Sandie Bello's relatives, who earns his living as one of the fisherman of the Bahamas Islands.

Onandi had remembered, when he was only five years of age, while being out on the beach shoreline of their town, with his Uncle Joel Ato; it would be Onandi's uncle, who then had told his nephew, if Onandi can look closer at the far out waters, surrounding the area of the island town, he could most likely see the sea creature. During the very same day, as he looked out at the crystal, clear waters around the area of the island town of the Bahamas, Onandi Bello had thought he had seen a slight *prehistoric* view, of the sea creature, before the old, giant lizard dipped back down into the deep sea.

"My father believes, the sea creature is for real," Jearl Allan says, as she waits along the shoreline with her two best friends. Jearl Allan's father works ,at one of the local offices, in downtown *Nassau*; at times Jearl's father would spend his other times, studying about if there is such a idea, as any ancient, sea creatures which could have, or perhaps are still in the waters around their town in the Bahamas.

As the warm winds, from the seas blow causing the air around the fishing town, to become even warmer, the three island children will just sit, and talk about their beautiful island, the Bahamas. While the three twelve year olds, Onandi and Sandie Bello, as Jearl Allan talk, suddenly the three twelve year olds will see something out in the waters, just some distances away, from where the three are just sitting, from hours of playing along the shorelines of the island town. The crystal blue waters, as the winds blow on; seems to show ripples on top of the crystal, blue waters.

The three island children, will next stand up; and while holding the twelve year olds gasp, suddenly all three; Onandi and Sandi Bello, with Jearl Allan; will suddenly see a view of something, which looks like—the sea creature. Then rapidly, *if it was,* the ancient, supposedly prehistoric animal, will just drop down back down in the deep, crystal blue waters of the Bahamas islands, unawares it has just been seen, by three curious island children. Later, the three island children will now have a good idea. Soon, there would be the season when tourists will be visiting their small town, located on one of the islands in the Bahamas. When the weather becomes just warm and pleasant enough, the small town in the Bahamas along with other islands around the Bahamas, will be flooded with tourists, it seems from all other areas of the world. Onandi and Sandie Bello, with their friend Jearl Allan; will set up a booth, for the tourists to have a glimpse of their fairy-tale monster, when and if the tourists would like to.

When the following morning had arrived, a lone fisherman by the name of Uncle Joel Ato is preparing to go out along the shoreline of the town where he lives; so he can prepare to fish, to fed as well as support his own family. Uncle Joel Ato had been an fisherman in his family, for as long as the aging islander can remember, also Uncle Joel Ato's own father and his father before his father; has always been fisherman on the island of the Bahamas.

For the same morning, Uncle Joel Ato did not ask his only nephew, Onandi to come along for the certain morning. Although Uncle Joel Ato, have enjoyed talking with his nephew Onandi about a fairy tale sea creature—Uncle Joel Ato, after so many years, at times believes his own island people, really do not believe if *Yamaly,* the *sea-dino* really exists. A belief Uncle Joel Ato will keep to him; is when he was just a boy of twelve years old; while being out with his own father, one warm, sunny day to fish; both Uncle Joel Ato and his father had actually seen the so-called—fairy tale sea creature.

While being out to fish, both Uncle Joel Ato, and his father, had the feeling of something such as like a huge, broken off trunk of an old palm tree, under their fishing boat. Uncle

Joel Ato then, had thought his father had caught one of the big *fish*, until Uncle Joel Ato and his father's boat was almost tumbled over. Uncle Joel Ato had thought the adventure to be fun, even though his father's boat was still intact; before both Uncle Joel Ato and his father set out to return back to the shorelines of his town; the twelve-year-old Joel Ato then; had glanced back. Suddenly, Uncle Joel Ato had seen the sea creature before it plunged its body back into the deep, blue sea around the island.

After Uncle Joel Ato, has finished with the preparations for his fishing for today, the islander hopes he has a good catch for today. As well, Uncle Joel Ato knew the tourist season for the small town of located in the Bahamas is going to be overcrowded with tourists. As Uncle Joel Ato, sits down on the beach close to his boat, the islander will see the same, ripples out on the waters around the beach shoreline. The ripples would go on and on, and then Uncle Joel Ato will narrow his eyes, to see if the *Yamaly, the sea-dino*—will appear. Next, the ripples would become less and less; then Uncle Joel Ato, will climb into his fishing boat, to begin perhaps a good day of fishing.

As the late evening settles around the small town in the Bahamas, Jearl Allen is now at home with her parents, and the Allen family are now enjoying a meal of two different sorts of island, smoked meats with plantains, one of the island of the Bahamas, most tasty food items. Jearl Allen also likes the time of being with her family, besides the evening meal; Jearl's father would be home, and she can just sit and talk to her father, who works at times, long hours at office, located in the area of the island.

"The food was good mama," Jearl Allen is now saying to her mother, as Mrs. Allen is now clearing the dining table from dishes, because the evening meal is now over. At the same moment, Jearl will ask her father Mr. Allen a question, about the so called, *Yamaly, the sea-dino.*

"Father, is it really true, there is a *prehistoric* monster, who lives out in the ocean, near our home?" Jearl Allen is asking, as her deep, brown eyes are becoming full of curiosity, then next her father Mr. Allen, will suggest why don't he and his only daughter Jearl, go out to the wide, wooden front porch of the Allen's home, to talk about a fairy tale sea creature.

After Jearl Allen and her father, are now out on the front porch of their home, both father and daughter, will sit on two islands chairs made of bamboo, which Mrs. Allen brought one day, at a local shop in *Nassau*. At the moment, the winds around the island of the Bahamas is blowing much cooler; also there is a full moon, casting its glow over the ocean waters, too the home of Jearl Allen and her family, are just several yards away from the view of the beach around the town in the Bahamas.

"So Jearl, you want to know about the *Yamaly*?" her father is asking his daughter, Jearl; as well, Mr. Allen is not at all surprised because of his daughter's question. Ever since he was just a boy of twelve, while living on the island too, Mr. Allen and the other children during those days would wait and wait, sometimes during the late evenings of the days around the island, on the shoreline of the beach, to wait and catch a look see for the fairy tale, sea creature.

"Yes father, my two friends has a fisherman in their family. He has told Onandi and Sandie, stories about the sea creature", Jearl talks on to say. Next, Mr. Allen will exhale, and then next tell his only daughter Jearl, just as much in detail, about the so-called make-believe sea creature, known as the *Yamaly, the sea-dino*. Mr. Allen only nods in agreement, and then he begins to tell his daughter Jearl about the make-believe sea creature, now known as the *Yamaly, the sea-dino*.

"Since the early days of our island, as well as the world, there had been certain animals, known as prehistoric dinosaurs, so it is said the giant lizards roamed the earth. You do know about prehistoric dinosaurs and the like, Jearl?" Mr. Allen is now asking, as he also has his daughter's full attention.

"Yes I do papa, we learned how the dinosaurs roamed the earth; until a meteor landed later the giant dinosaurs were no longer," Jearl is now saying, and she is about to become excited as her father talks.

"Well, there are some folks believe the dinosaurs never did live, then there others who believed they actually did", Mr. Allen says.

"Does it mean; the *Yamaly,* sea creature could have lived in the ocean waters around our island?" Jearl asks, and she can notice the moon high up into the skies above the island of the

Bahamas, is showing brighter and brighter.

"There are not many facts Jearl, yet I can remember as a small boy, just about your age; my friends during those days; had believed the sea creature had lived," Mr. Allen says, also he is finding the moment to talk to his only daughter, to be rather nice.

"The Yamaly, is really a *sea creature*?" Jearl has now asked, and she hopes what she has asked her father; he would say, *"Yes"*.

"From the time, when I was a boy; we were told the fable, the sea creature known as the *Yamaly*, has a long-shaped mouth, a long neck, and flippers on his huge body," Mr. Allen now says, yet he hopes he is not being overly untrue with his only daughter Jearl. Right now, Jearl's eyes are now focused, on the wide scene of the shoreline, not too far from her family's home; suddenly Jearl Allen can imagine the sea creature—even as her father speaks.

When both father and daughter are finished talking, Jearl and Mr. Allen are walking back inside, also it is becoming late in the evening. Jearl Allen, after she prepares to go to bed, will walk over to the window of her bedroom, and just stare out to the endless stretch of the ocean waters, which surrounds the small town of the island of the Bahamas. Even if her eyes are becoming tired, and Jearl wants to sleep, yet before she climbs into her bed; Jearl Allen had thought she had seen the top front of a *whatever*, show up way out far from the shoreline. Jearl will go to bed believing, she may have seen the sea creature, *known as the Yamaly.*

As the winds continue to blow, swishing the full leaves of the palm trees, which dot the area along the shoreline of the Bahamas, Onandie and Sandie Bello, are sitting outside their own front porches of their homes, and the Bello family has just completed their evening meal of smoked fish, along with plantains too. Onandie and Sandie had asked to go outside and talk, while their Uncle Joel Ato, talks to both twelve year olds parents, about his good catch, from fishing earlier of the morning.

While Onandie and Sandie are sitting, out on chairs which the two twelve year olds father, had shaped out of a sturdy wood, of the island of Bahamas; it would be Onandie who will start the talk between him and his sister Sandie. Before both twelve year olds, even sat down to have an evening meal with their family, Onandie Bello had wanted to go out to the beach, yet he could not. Onandie must have his evening meal with his family; and it is an honor too for his family, to have their Uncle Joel Ato to be at the Bello's house. As the moon shines brighter, Sandie will ask her brother what he thinks of the sea creature—known as the *Yamaly, the sea-dino really*.

"Our Uncle Joel Ato thinks *it* is for *real*. He told me, one day as he and I were fishing, Uncle Joel Ato had seen it when he was just as boy my age," Onandi Bello is now saying, as he keeps his twelve year old gaze, right out to the shoreline and the wide ocean, surrounding the island of the Bahamas where the Bello family lives.

"I hope it's real, I want to see the sea creature. I don't think it will harm us, or the other people who live on our island," Sandie says, as she too keeps her gaze out to the shoreline and ocean.

"I tell you what, before the tourists visit our island, we can perhaps see the *sea monster known as Yamaly*. Then next, we can tell others, so we can have the tourists to pay, to see it", Onandi says, although he is right now unsure, as to what he has just replied to his younger sister Sandie.

"I don't know if we can what if the sea creature is just a fable, from what our people who had lived on the islands before us believes?" Sandie Bello now says, yet she believes though, the *Yamaly* known as the sea monster; is most likely a real, ancient animal.

"We shall see, tomorrow we will meet our friend Jearl, and wait again on the beach," Onandie says, then next both brother and sister, will hear their own mother, calling for them to now come back inside of the home. Before Onandie and Sandie, walks back inside; they would meet their Uncle Joel Ato, who is on his way out, to go home, from another day of fishing, for his family. Ahead of Uncle Joel Ato, going to his own home, it would be Onandie who will ask his uncle, if he had seen the *Yamaly* while Uncle Joel Ato, was out to catch fish for the day.

"Not today young Onandie," Uncle Joel Ato, will reply in his old, island accent. "But someone will see it soon," the uncle lastly say, then he walks on in the late evening, smiling as his twelve year old, niece and nephew are still standing outside their home;

perhaps wondering what Uncle Joel Ato has said; would really become true. All the while, as Uncle Joel Ato, and his family, is preparing to end their day; the sea creature known as the *Yamaly* is now close to the seashores, trying to rest its weary, prehistoric fins.

CHAPTER 2

Although the Bahamas is really a nation of more than three thousand, small and not so small islands, surrounded by coastal reefs and inlets, the Bahamas is located in the Atlantic Ocean, and the island has a warm, tropical atmosphere all year long. Beautiful yellow flowers, can be seen around the islands of the Bahamas, along with various kinds of palm trees, which can be seen throughout the islands, also different exotic birds with local bay fish areas, is where the local island people can catch fish, usually for their own to sell in local markets. For sure, when a person foot touches the sandy beaches, there are so many scenic sights about the islands of the Bahamas. The small town along the sun and fun of the island will have more visitors wanting to visit a well-known one, which has a fairy tale of a sea creature, which can be seen at times from the area. Make-believe stories would surround the islands of the Bahamas, mostly because of a fable about a sea monster, known as the *Yamaly,* which has been seen by some other local people of the islands.

Soon, as the visitors get ready to arrive to the islands of the Bahamas, three twelve-year olds, who are also best friends; are going to think of some ways perhaps Onandi and Sandi Bello, and their friend also Jearl Allen; will set out one day to maybe see the *Yamaly;* a sea creature who the three island children has heard, many fables about the *prehistoric* like animal. The three best friends, Onandi and Sandi Bello, also Jearl Allen; hopes they can assist the visitors, so they can catch a peep of the *Yamaly*. Then again, the three island children, must first try for their own being, to find out if the sea creature is real; as well Onandi and

Sandi Bello, with Jearl Allen just as the fairy tales has foretold of the sea creature.

When a new morning has arrived on the island of the Bahamas, two other fishermen has decided to go out, and catch fish for their own market wares. Although the two island men, are very much aware of the fairy tale about some sea creature, the two fishermen will just overlook the stories; all because of the years both fishermen has been out into the deep, crystal blue waters around the islands of the Bahamas, has never seen the make-believe sea creature, known as *Yamaly*. After the two fishermen, has checked to find out if their fishing gear is intact, they will climb into their usual near, old sail boat, then head out to the sea, yet not to far; to being their day's work of fishing.

While fishing, it would be the first fisherman, who as he keeps his almost old fishing rod, thrown out alongside the near old sail boat, begins to wonder if he and his other fishing friend would catch any fish for today. As the sun, slowly inches its way, high up into the skies above the islands of the Bahamas, both fishermen after almost two hours; began to lose hope because of not being able to catch any fish for the day. Suddenly, when the second fisherman suggests to the other fisherman, both should just go home and try for another warm day, to catch fish, both fishermen will feel their near old fishing boat, rocks as if it is going to plainly tumble over into the crystal, blue waters of the islands.

"*Say Mon*, what is going on here?" the first fisherman asks, with his island accent, as his friend who came along, begins to wonder as well.

"We must have gone out to far, the boat is starting to *shake Mon*," the second fisherman says, as he tries to keep a steady hand on his own fishing rod, yet it would do no good for the second fisherman. All because, the more their near, old sail boat rocks, the second fisherman will rapidly lose his own fishing rod.

"Let's try to row back *mon*, I don't like the feel of this one," the first fisherman says, then next as the two island fishermen begin to try and row their almost, old sail boat, back to the seashore; both fishermen will feel their near old sailing boat, seems to lift up almost four feet up in the air, as if something is causing the near, old sail boat to do so.

As the two fishermen, begin to wonder as well become a little alarmed, swiftly their near old sail boat, while still up almost four feet in the air; will very fast began to move itself, faster and faster until both fisherman, have landed with a hard and sudden bump, on the shores of the beach. When the two fishermen, after landing safely on the shore of the beach, will look at each other, until the first fisherman asks his fishing friend, what was *it*, which pushed their near old sail boat out of the waters around the island?

"I don't known *mon*, must have been the wind," the second fisherman says, next when both fishermen has gotten out of their near old sail boat, all of a sudden; the two fishermen will hear a wailing sound, almost like the sound of a whale. Next, the two fishermen will take a quick peek, to see from across to the far side of the beach; will be some creature, with a long neck, flippers like a dolphin, and a long, top front; and huge, slant like bright eyes. After the *sea creature*, stops its watch on the two fishermen, it would waddle back into the crystal, blue waters, leaving a trail in the sand, from where it had stood, from its huge fins.

At the time, when the two anglers had returned back to their own town, they would try and tell the other islanders, just what they had possibly seen—the sea monster known as the *Yamaly*. The two fishermen would also find the two of them, in arguments about their truth, even though the two fishermen had been told about the fairy-tale, sea creature ever since the two fishermen were both young children. Until later, the two fishermen would wait until some months later, before either of the two ever ventures out into the ocean, around the islands of the Bahamas.

When another sunny, bright morning arrives around the islands of the Bahamas, three island children; Onandi and Sandi Bello, also Jearl Allen, will set out to play about on the sandy beaches, yet not too far from their own homes; but far enough because the three island children have a plan, to try and catch a peek at the *Yamaly*, the sea creature. All three-island children heard their own parents, talk about the two anglers, who had stated to see the *Yamaly*. After hearing the story, Jearl Allen could not hardly sleep during the very same night, all because she and her other two friends, wants to see the sea creature known as the *Yamaly*.

While the three island twelve-year olds, are out and about on the sandy beach; Onandi Bello will see a conch shell, left abandon on the beach, just as many of the others which the island children had seen various of times. After getting the conch shell, Onandi will blow into the empty conch shell; suddenly all three will notice the abandon conch shell, which looks to be almost the size of a basketball, has the sound of a *horn*.

"Maybe we can use the shell, as a signal for the *Yamaly*," Jearl Allen says, as both of her two other friends agree, then next all three island children, will walk just a little closer to the edge of the sandy beach. While being there, and as he holds on to the conch shell, Onandi will do just as Jearl has suggested; then as he inhales deeply to blow into the empty conch shell, the three children will just stand close to the water's edge; then wait.

"I hope he can hear us, under the ocean," Sandi now says, and then her brother Onandi will blow harder into the empty conch shell. Then something will all of sudden happen, for the three, curious island children. From the edge of the beach, where the three are standing, the waters will next begin to ripple with medium, sized waves. With their deep, brown eyes becoming deep in thought, the ripples would become even more in full view; next when Onandi Bello blows again into the empty clam shell, the three island children are going to witness a sight, which all of them had wondered if the fairy tale, in view of a certain sea creature—is actually *true*.

In the middle of the ripples of the ocean waters, what has been only a fairy tale, since the start of the islands of the Bahamas' history; will be the so named *Yamaly*-the sea creature. Although the three island children, are almost afraid, there would be small voices in the rear of their curious mindsets; telling Onandi and Sandi Bello, also Jearl Allen the prehistoric sea creature, is just as harmless as a *dolphin*. The three island children, would just see only the top front of the *Yamaly*, also as it looks at the area of the beach, where the three children are standing; the *Yamaly* appears to be just as curious as the humans by standing, three twelve year olds on the beach.

"Is it really the *Yamaly*?" Jearl Allen will ask, as the sea creature continues its stay, just showing its top front as well also its long neck. At the same moment, the three island children can hear a not to loud, yet soft sound much like a whale one, clearly being heard from the *Yamaly*.

"It is, and he looks sad," Sandi Bello says, as the sea creature keeps bobbing its top front, then lastly it would plunge back down into the ocean waters, lastly the ripples would slowly die down from the *Yamaly's* fading from the three island children's sights.

"He's not dangerous at all, not like the way our people has said," Onandi says, then next it would be Jearl who will say another idea, to her two friends, who along with Jearl Allen, has just had their first glimpse of the *Yamaly*, the *sea-dino*.

"Let's keep this our secret, and the next time; let us bring *Yamaly* some food, such as fish," Jearl Allen says, then when her other two friends agree with Jearl; the three island children will go about their playing, also it would be Onandi who will keep the empty conch shell, next to his bedside of his home. Onandi and Sandi Bello's parents, would not question why their son, wants to keep a hold onto the conch shell. Such items are known throughout, the entire islands of the Bahamas.

During a new sunny morning, Uncle Joel Ato had decided to go out again and catch some more fish. As he gets all of his fishing gear together, Uncle Joel Ato is not afraid to go out on the ocean waters. The near old islander had heard about the stories of the two fishermen, who had claimed to see the *Yamaly*. Uncle Joel Ato knew for all the years of living on the islands of the Bahamas; no one has really seen the sea creature known as the *Yamaly*. Then again, Uncle Joel Ato knew other fables surrounding the sea creature. Uncle Joel Ato, knew even as a young child, the local islanders, such as if the sea creature really exists; only come out into view on a full moonlit night, surfing the ocean waters around the islands of the Bahamas.

Uncle Joel Ato, also knew of the old story about his people who had at one time believed in a not to true image, known as the *Yamalla*—a West Indies ancient not real island *sprite*, who controls actions of the moon at night, and who the *Yamalla* lives in the deep, chrystal blue ocean waters around the islands of the Bahamas. These days, the local islanders really do not believe if there ever has been neither a *Yamalla*— nor a sea creature known as the *Yamaly*. As Uncle Joel Ato, sits in his own sail boat, after setting it out not to far from the seashore of the beach, he begins to think just how much fun it had been when Uncle Joel Ato, had been told some exciting stories about the sea creature.

After three hours of Uncle Joel Ato, out catching fishes not too far from the seashore, he would have more than enough fishes for his family, as well as some of the fishes to take to the local market, if Uncle Joel Ato wants to. As he slowly rows his sail boat, back to the seashore, as he lifts out his heavy load of fishes, Uncle

Joel Ato is very much unawares he is being watched, by the so named, prehistoric sea creature known as the *Yamaly*. As the sun slowly begins to set on the very same day, the sea creature would just swim its huge body, which is only twenty-foot long, across the ocean waters, always plunging its top front, until it has a mouthful of some of the fishes. Up till now, before the *Yamaly* sets out to go farther out into the ocean waters, it would look back at the seashore—as if the *Yamaly* is expecting three, curious island twelve-year olds, the sea creature had seen earlier.

CHAPTER 3

200 million years ago, the world was then created of a huge, yet single land mass, then as time goes by for millions of years more; the huge masses of land would break off to form mostly continents. Then, there

would be some giant animals around during those millions of years, known as *dinosaurs*. Some people even today, view *dinosaurs* as huge monsters, when the animals roamed the earth some millions of years earlier. These giant monsters would be later known to be terrible lizards, because of the built of those animals. It is even known, that the terrible, giant lizards, had lived on every continent of the world. There would be in the present time, bones as well as fossils found in different parts of the world, to suggest the giant monsters had lived.

No one can really claim, why these giant lizards had become no longer. Some believed the swamps and lagoons where the *dinosaurs* could have lived were drained and the huge lizards died. Some people believed, when the climates and vegetations, changed quickly; the change was not too well for the *dinosaurs*, and they all may have died just because. Until today, a small town located on one of the islands of Bahamas, there would be many of make-believe stories, about a sea creature known as *Yamaly*, only appeared when there is bright light, of a full moon shines on the ocean around the islands, a person may see the *Yamaly*. Even if some of the fairy stories are true about the *Yamaly*, three island children, Onandi and Sandi Bello, also Jearl Allen, being good friends, had gone out one day to the seashores out along from their homes, to the *Yamaly* for the first time.

Mr. and Mrs. Allen would soon be awake from the sound of their only daughter's scream, while Jearl was trying to fall asleep one night. It would be Mrs. Allen though, who will agree to walk quickly into her daughter's bedroom, to find out what is troubling Jearl so late in the night. After Mrs. Allen is now in her daughter's bedroom, she can right now see Jearl is wide-awake, perhaps from a terrible dream, which Jearl just had.

"My child, what is the matter?" Mrs. Allen is asking Jearl, in her island accent, and Mrs. Allen is now sitting down on the bed near her daughter.

"I had a dream, it was not bad; yet it still scared me mama," Jearl is now saying, and she seems to be out of her twelve-year old breath.

"Tell me about it Jearl," Mrs. Allen now says, then as she sits on and listens to Jearl talk about the dream, from what her daughter has just dreamed; Mrs. Allen believes Jearl's dreams could be from the make-believe stories Uncle Joel Ato, has been telling about the island sea creature known as the *Yamaly*.

Mrs. Allen has always known about the make-believe sea creature, even when she was just a child, of the same age as her only daughter Jearl is right now, Mrs. Allen never did believe there ever was such a creature. Mrs. Allen nowadays, view the stories about the *Yamaly*, as some island folk tale, mostly for the visitors who had spend time at the islands of the Bahamas, during mostly the early times of winter. When Jearl is finished talking about her almost terrible dream, Mrs. Allen will assure Jearl what has just awaken her, is only just as; a dream.

"So you see child, the *Yamaly* was only a dream, no one knows if it's really out there in the ocean," Mrs. Allen says, next Jearl will ask her mother a question, concerning the sea creature.

"Do you believe *Yamaly*, is for real?" Jearl asks, her deep brown eyes widening, even if one sunny day, Jearl and her two friends, had believed they had seen the *Yamaly*.

"Well my dear child Jearl, when I ever see the *Yamaly*, I want you to be with me; then we can both believe," is all Mrs. Allen says, then after she kisses Jearl good-night again, promising her only daughter, there would be no more awful dreams, soon Jearl Allen is falling asleep again.

When the new morning arrives, Jearl Allen hardly could eat her breakfast of sweet rolls and island plantains, even if she had a terrible dream about a so named sea creature; still Jearl Allen wants to have another chance to see the sea creature, with her other two friends. After she arrives to the area to meet her two friends, Jearl Allen can also see, not only her two friends Onandi and Sandi Bello are there waiting, today along the seashore has some visitors there.

"They are here to see the *Yamaly*," Onandi is saying to Jearl, as she is walking near where her two friends are standing, which is just a few yards away from the visitors. Jearl Allen had totally forgotten, about the visitors, who at times visited the islands of the Bahamas; especially to catch a glimpse of the famous sea creature, which is about to gain as much attention as the *Loch Ness of Scotland*.

"I hope they don't stay long, I want to see the *Yamaly* today," Sandi Bello is now saying, as she looks too at the visitors, with their cameras and *binoculars*, all pointing out to the ocean for the *Yamaly* to do an appearance. After it seems as if the visitors to the islands, has been there almost hours; soon the visitors would be walking away from the seashore; one by one, all seeming to be disappointed. When Onandi, Sandi and Jearl, has seen the visitors are now gone away, it would be Onandi who will go and get his conch shell the size almost of a basketball, to blow out and signal the *Yamaly*.

As the three friends, stand and wait; the sun seems to be getting ready to set; almost casting shades of light orange and blue over the horizon, across the oceans. Next, Onandi will blow even harder into the empty conch shell, and then the three island children will finally have their chance, to view a giant lizard, which lives in the sea, which has really been known to be just a fairy story. While standing ever so still, close to the edge of the seashore; yet not too far out into the wide ocean waters, all of a sudden the same ripples of from the ocean will be seen by Onandi, Sandi, and Jearl.

The three island twelve-year olds are about to become too excited, because as the ripples of ocean water began to rise up just slightly; from afar where Sandi, Jearl and Onandi are standing along the seashore; the top front of the sea creature, can already be seen. The three island friends, keep their silence, as the *Yamaly* just appears to be just bobbing its top front , and then Jearl, Sandi and Onandi, are now waving at the sea creature, as if the ancient animal can understand the young twelve-year olds, along on the beach.

"It doesn't seem to be dangerous", is all Jearl says, as the sea creature keeps its own curious, *prehistoric* eyes on the young, twelve-year old children.

"We better not go too far out in the ocean. I wonder if it's hungry." Onandi says, and then it would be his younger sister, who reminds the both Jearl and her brother Onandi, they did not bring anything for the *Yamaly* to eat.

"I wish we had some fishes, the *Yamaly* is still waiting, as if we can feed it," Jearl is now saying, as the sea creature keeps bobbing its front top above the ocean, as if it is still wondering just who is standing on the beach.

"My Uncle Joel Ato has some fishes in one of his tanks, which is close to our home. We can go there quickly, and return for the *Yamaly*," Onandi has now said, then as the three island children go off to get some fishes; when they finally return with only a pail full; the sea creature known as the *Yamaly*, cannot be seen.

"It's gone," Sandi will say, with a feeling of sadness.

"We can come back tomorrow. We will leave the fishes in the pail, let us not tell our parents about seeing the Yamaly," Jearl Allen says, then as the sun starts to go down slowly; the three island friends, has promised they will return another day, to feed their *brand new* sea creature. Of course, the three island children, has another idea in mind, as to the *Yamaly*. Then again, to do what Onandi, Sandi and Jearl has in their young twelve-year old minds, could be dangerous, yet they all want to actually have an even closer look at the *Yamaly*; even though by now all three believe there is really a sea creature, who lives in the ocean around their islands of the Bahamas.

The day when the three island children, had seen the *Yamaly*; Uncle Joel Ato was busy selling his goods of fishes, which he had caught some days before. Uncle Joel Ato knew, when the visitors arrive to the islands of the Bahamas, some of them wanted to have an island taste, of the various seafood he would catch. As well, Uncle Joel Ato, knew some of the visitors to the islands, had really came to catch a glimpse of the *Yamaly*, which has been told and re-told since Uncle Joel Ato was a small boy, living on the island.

It did not surprise Uncle Joel Ato, when the day he had been out fishing, he had not seen not one sighting of the *Yamaly*. As he casted his nets and other fishing gear among the wide ocean, there were not any ripples, and the only real sea life Uncle Joel Ato had seen, where the playful dolphins, besides his other fishes which he had caught. When he was finished with selling his seafood at the market, Uncle Joel Ato would return to his own home, although he had plans to visit his family. While standing on his wide, wooden porch; Uncle Joel Ato would just stare out at the wide ocean; then all of a sudden; Uncle Joel Ato had thought he had heard a sound, which also sounds like a whale from a distance, coming way from across the ocean.

As the near old fisherman, keeps still on his wide, wooden porch; the sound which is coming from the ocean, can be heard yet not too loud; Uncle Joel Ato believes even now, the *Yamaly* must be drawing closer to the seashore of the islands. As the wailing sound, though not too somber continues, Uncle Joel Ato will glance up at the night sky, and sees not only the *Ursa Major*, or *Big Dipper* and the smaller one; the near aging fisherman can see there is a full moon out tonight. Even now, Uncle Joel Ato is starting to feel tired, perhaps because of his day at the market. Then after he walks back into his own house, while the sounds maybe from the sea creature continues on; Uncle Joel Ato will go to sleep, thinking perhaps he just may have his chance to see the *Yamaly*; except not for the certain night as of now.

When the dark of the night becomes even later, the sea creature that has been living out in the ocean waters around a certain island, will waddles its *prehistoric* clumsy body, just close enough to the seashores of the island. Since the dawn of time, the ancient sea creature has always lugged its body just close enough, to breathe into an unusual scent of air, and relax only its old body. The sea creature though, is unawares it is now a subject of folk stories as well as make-believe, even though the sea creature has been noticed, by three curious island children.

Its not as if the sea creature has not seen humans ever before, yet when it does waddle just close enough to the seashore, which is usually on a full moonlit night, or whenever the seashore along the beach is almost empty; it is then the sea creature just lays still as the ocean waves seem to wash it's too old, *dinosaur like* body. Because of its prehistoric habits, the sea creature too will keep his ancient, eyes just open enough to be sure, there will no harm done to its *prehistoric* body. There has not been hardly any food, for the sea creature to eat; except only the fishes and perhaps other sea life, which is way smaller for the sea creature to eat. After minutes of just it seems as if the *Yamaly* is sleeping, before the ancient giant animal, waddles back into the ocean, it would notice something on the seashore.

When the sea creature has waddled close enough to a pail of fresh fishes, the prehistoric sea creature will topple over the pail of seafood, with the top front of its body. Then next, the sea creature will begin to eat, the now dead fresh fishes, while at the same time lifting up the top front of its body, as if the *dinosaur* is being watchful. After the *Yamaly*, has its full of the seafood, it would next waddle back into the ocean depths. When the dawn of the morning arrives, the pail of fishes is now empty, and the ocean tide has washed away the fin like prints, which was dotted along the seashore.

CHAPTER 4

As she is sitting with her two parents, one morning for breakfast, Jearl Allen will hear the very way her mother and father, are talking about the *Yamaly*. Ever since she and her two best friends, Onandi and Sandi Bello, had actually seen the sea creature, Jearl Allen has been very careful not to really tell her parents.

Even if Jearl at times enjoys the stories, her own father had told her about the Yamaly; Jearl Allen mostly because she and her two best friends own curiosity, had wanted to see at least the sea creature for their own likings.

Sometimes as she is in her own bedroom during the late evenings, Jearl Allen will think about the *Yamaly*, even how sad the sea creature had appeared. As well, Jearl and her two best friends, also views the sea creature as totally harmless, because of its sad look. When her two parents are now finished talking about the *Yamaly*, and how the way the tourists are now on the islands of the Bahamas, just because, Jearl Allen now must prepare to go to the market with her mother.

After arriving to the market, the area is crowded as usual, and Jearl Allen will keep quiet and walk along with her mother, as she thinks about what Jearl and her two best friends, Onandi and Sandi Bello, has planned. As her mother look closely at the various foods to buy, among other items such as fabrics of bright colors, Jearl Allen will see some of the people at the market, are wearing brightly colored t-shirts with a picture supposedly of the *Yamaly*. Jearl Allen, also because of her curious twelve-year old mind, only had to guess the persons wearing the brightly colored t-shirts, must be the visitors who are visiting the islands of the Bahamas.

"We are finished, are you ready Jearl?' her mother is now asking, after paying for the various items, and when Jearl signals to her mother, she is more than ready; suddenly both Jearl and her mother Mrs. Allen will come close to two people, a elderly man and woman, who could be just visitors who are visiting the islands of the Bahamas. Jearl and her mother would only look curious, before the elderly man will ask the islanders a question, concerning the *Yamaly*.

"Excuse me, I do not intend to impose, my wife and I are wondering, if you by any chance has seen the sea-dino, the *Yamaly*?" the elderly man asks, and Jearl and her mother Mrs. Allen, sees he has a camera around his neck.

"I believe my daughter Jearl can answer your question," Mrs. Allen says, then as the elderly couple looks at Jearl, next Mrs. Allen will give her daughter the signal, perhaps the two persons are only tourists, then Jearl will answer the question.

"The *Yamaly* has been a legend among our people for a long time", is all Jearl Allen says, and then she and her mother will walk on, leaving behind the elderly tourist couple, somewhat satisfied, in what Jearl has said.

"Well said, my dear child," Mrs. Allen says in her own island accent, and then both mother and daughter would soon be home, so Jearl Allen can go outside and meet her two best friends.

Although Jearl Allen, has really seen the *Yamaly*; with her two best friends, she has been very careful as not to really tell her own parents. Jearl also knows, some older persons such as her parents, usually views young kids like Jearl and her two best friends, to have a run wild of thoughts. A belief Jearl Allen is really for certain, she has seen the Yamaly; the sea creature is alive and well; also she and her two best friends, Onandi and Sandi Bello, could be the only persons who has *actually* seen the sea creature.

After she arrives to the area, of the seashore, Jearl Allen will see her two best friends, and Sandi Bello is holding the empty pail in her right hand. As she walks closer, Jearl Allen can recall, the pail was full of fishes, which they all had for the *Yamaly* to eat. Even though the pail of fishes is empty, Jearl Allen can see her two best friends, are happier as well as very much awaiting to see the *Yamaly*, even if all three have to go and find more fishes for the sea creature.

"It has been here, look Jearl the fishes are gone!" Sandi says, and now the three twelve-year olds know what they must do, to have another look-see for the *Yamaly*.

"We have to go and catch some more fishes, if he comes back again," Onandi says, then as the three go and find something to catch at least a few of the fishes; when they do; all three twelve-year olds cannot until all of sudden there is a fishing pole lying on the seashore, where all three are standing.

"Maybe one of the fishermen who lives around the islands, has left it behind," Jearl says, and then she and her two best friends are on their way close to the ocean, as they can, so they try to catch at least some fishes. To do so, it would be Onandi who decides to go just so into the water; and he next tells Sandi and Jearl to stay on the seashore, so Onandi can *"fish."* As he prepares the fishing rod to fish, all three-island children will notice the same ripples of waves, which are trying to form as Onandi tries to catch some seafood for the *Yamaly*.

"Look Jearl, the waves are trying to come back," Sandi says, as she keeps also her eyes on her brother, who is still trying to catch some fishes. At the moment, both Sandi and Jearl knows perhaps why the ripples of the ocean waves, are trying to appear again. Too at the same moment, Onandi has caught at least four good sized fishes, then all of sudden the three twelve-year olds, will see the sea creature, this time only just it seems, three hundred yards are so, from where Jearl, Sandi and Onandi Bello are standing along the seashore.

"Look there it is!" shouts Sandi, until the *Yamaly*, next dips his top front back down in the ocean waters.

"Come on Onandi, before it gets too close!" shouts Jearl, even though she is about to feel as if she is going to *faint*. Right now, Onandi has ran up on the seashore, next as his sister and their best friend Jearl looks on, Onandi with all of his twelve-year old strength, will all of a sudden toss out the fish, almost one at a time, at the *Yamaly*.

What will happen at the same moment, will have the three island children; Sandi, Jearl and Onandi, laughing and almost dancing along the seashore, as the sea creature known as the *Yamaly*, leaps up its *prehistoric* body to catch the fishes, which Onandi has just thrown to the sea creature. Then next, because of the leap of the *Yamaly*, there is almost an eight-foot high wave of ocean water, yet not too high for the three island children; just enough to splatter them all totally wet. Later, the *Yamaly* after looking back at the three twelve-year olds, will swim back farther into the ocean, from where it had came; next when Sandi, Jearl and Onandi keeps their eyes on the ocean waters, they will catch a look see, as the sea creatures' tail suddenly vanishes.

When she returns home, Jearl Allen also her two best friends,

Onandi and Sandi Bello, will have one good excuse as to why their clothing are so wet. The three island children have told their parents, they had been enjoying a day of swimming just because. After having her evening meal, Jearl Allen will go to her bedroom and just daydream on and on, until bedtime about what has happened to Jearl and her, two best friends, from a day on the beach. As well, for the same night, Jearl Allen will not have any more bad dreams, and she cannot wait until another day, for both she and her two best friends. Before Jearl and her friend, Onandi and Sandi Bello, had gone home for the day; it would be Sandi who had seen a boat, with two oars alongside the seashore. All three, now have a new plan to meet and greet the well - known *sea-dino*, of the islands of the Bahamas, the *Yamaly*.

During the same night, Uncle Joel Ato had decided to go and walk along the seashore, something he has always enjoyed, ever since Uncle Joel Ato was a boy. It was also at the times, when Uncle Joel Ato had heard fairy stories after fairy stories, about the sea creature, which is about to have the islands of the Bahamas, to become fairly famous. Even though he had seen the sea creature known as the *Yamaly*, at those times, Uncle Joel Ato had believed it was only the moon image of long ago of his islands, known as the *Yamalla*.

Nowadays, Uncle Joel Ato knows no one really believes in the ancient, *Yamalla*, mostly because the younger islanders would rather have some sea creature, which just may really exist. As he walks on, the warm island winds, blowing against his face; Uncle Joel Ato wishes right now he can just stay on the seashore; then next a full moon will appear, through wispy, clouds which are now too in the skies above the islands of the Bahamas. Right now, Uncle Joel Ato will find a nice area to sit down, after he does; Uncle Joel Ato believe his near aging hearing is playing tricks on him — again.

As he sits on and listens, Uncle Joel Ato can faintly hear the sad, wailing of the sea creature, which is all too common to him. Even if the sound is known, Uncle Joel Ato knows the sea creature known by some islanders as the *Yamaly*, is anything but sad. As the sound goes on, Uncle Joel Ato will keep his gaze right out towards the ocean, perhaps where the sound is really coming from. While sitting, the near old fisherman of the islands, will see more clearly, the top front of the *Yamaly*, except now it seems to be swimming farther out into the ocean. Uncle Joel Ato, now stands up to go home, also as the sea creature keeps swimming on; the ripples of the ocean waves seems to be coming closer to Uncle Joel Ato, as he keeps walking home.

When the morning had arrived, for Jearl Allen to meet up with her two best friends, Onandi and Sandi Bello; she is about to almost shout with joy, mainly become of the plans Jearl and her two friends has for today. The night before, and just before she had gone to bed; Jearl Allen had spent some time reading about various stories about so-called *sea monsters*, which had been seen from different places in the area, all by so-called *experts*.

A certain story, which Jearl had read, was one about a so-called sea monster known as the *Loch Ness*. As she read in the past, Jearl Allen will find out, the so-called *Loch Ness*, or

Nessie, has been told in poems as well as created into different movies in regards. An added notion Jearl has noticed about the so- called *Loch Ness*, it seems to be the same identical as the *Yamaly*, which is known around the islands of the Bahamas.

After she arrives to the seashore, Jearl Allen can see her two best friends, Sandi and Onandi Bello are already there. It seems too, her two best friends have another pail of fresh fishes, to feed the *Yamaly*, if and when the sea creature comes back. As well, Jearl can see her two best friends, are near the boat with the two oars, and after she greets Sandi and Onandi Bello, the three island children will now begin, there new plan to have a much closer look-see at the *Yamaly*.

"I think we should only go out so far, at least we may be able to still see it," Onandi says, also he knows the ocean waters around the islands of the Bahamas, can be very dangerous; also, Onandi knows he and his sister Sandi, with Jearl must be careful.

"We can steer the oars, to be sure we do not go out too far," is what Jearl Allen says, even though she knows how to swim, yet Jearl has been cautioned by her own two parents, to not go out to near to the ocean waters. Next, the three island friends will slowly climb into the boat with the two oars, which they had found just a day ago. As Onandi and Jearl, slowly row the boat, while Sandi keeps her embrown eyes, on the surface of the waters, all of sudden, the three island children will feel the boat as if it is floating out rather *fast*.

"Don't row to fast Onandi, so we do not go too far out!", Jearl almost yells at Onandi, next he assures Jearl he is not hardly at all *rowing* the boat.

"Why does it feel, as you and Jearl are still rowing the boat?" Sandi asks, with a little thrill in her voice, and just a tiny bit of fear though.

"Let's try to turn back, so we don't float way out; we can leave the fishes for the *Yamaly*, on the seashore again, if we have to," Jearl Allen says, also at the same moment, the three island children, will all of a sudden feel the boat float on faster and faster.

"What is happening?" Onandi is asking, and he is really starting to feel a little scared.

"I don't know; let's row back faster and faster!" Jearl is now yelling, almost at the top of her twelve-year old lungs. Next, as the boat goes faster yet not to fast; the three island children will notice the giant front of the *Yamaly* with its wailing sounds as before, and it seems to be pulling their boat towards the seashore.

"There it is! There it is!" Jearl is shouting, except she is not afraid as her two best friends, then as the three island children, can see, the *Yamaly* is trying to help them back on dry land;

they all are laughing as their boat, while on the back of the *Yamaly*, sways a little to and fro; as the sea creature swims closer to the seashore.

"YEAAAAA!" all three are shouting with delight, until their boat is just close enough to the seashore, then the sea creature will emerge its top front, as well as its twenty-five feet long body, back down into the ocean; leaving the three island children floating slowly towards the seashore.

When their boat, has finally been set on the seashore, Sandi, Jearl and Onandi will look fast at the sea creature, and they will all notice its two fins, along with its twenty-five feet long body, then its tail fin, dipping in and out of the ocean waters, until it finally disappears. The three island twelve-year olds are calling out to the *Yamaly*, and waving *good-bye* to it. As well the three best friends, have been having such fun of being close to the sea creature, Sandi, Jearl and Onandi are unawares their pail of fishes is now empty, as well as still in their boat.

CHAPTER 5

Although it has been months it seems, as if the two fishermen who had seen the *Yamaly*, has been out on the ocean waters, around their village located in the islands of the Bahamas; the two fishermen after telling all the stories about seeing the *Yamaly*, it seems as if no one would believe the two fishermen. Besides being out to fish on that certain day, the two anglers had noticed they had not caught any fish during that moment. Now, the two anglers want to go out, to find, as well as have another look see to find the *Yamaly*.

When the day had arrived, both anglers while being out along the seashore to begin their plans, to go out into the ocean, have noticed there are not many tourists out and around the seashore. The two fishermen, also knows for the season; there are a lot of visitors who are now on the islands of the Bahamas, also the two fishermen hopes to capture some pictures of the *Yamaly*. Both island fishermen have plans to sell some of the pictures of the *Yamaly*, also to prove to some other islanders they had actually seen the sea creature.

After setting up their near old boat, both fishermen are now sailing along out to the ocean; yet not too far, just because. The warm, tropical winds are blowing, as the two fishermen one with a near old camera, and the other one; has a long, sharp fishing spear with plans to take a hit at the sea creature. As their both keeps sailing along, the same ripples on the ocean waters, are starting to become obvious, as the two fishermen believes the ripples could be a good sign, the *Yamaly* is not too far from where they are in the boat.

"Do you see it *mon*?" the first one of the fishermen, is asking the other one; as the second fisherman keeps his eyes on the ocean for some sign of the *Yamaly*. Both fishermen knew of the sea-dino, they too had heard make-believe stories about a very giant, lizard, which lives in and around the ocean waters of the islands of the Bahamas. Neither of the two fishermen, had really believed the *Yamaly* actually exists, all became both of the fishermen when they were young boys, they only thought the sea creature story was merely a bedtime story for years and years, around the islands of the Bahamas.

As the two fishermen's boat keeps sailing along, also as the ripples on the ocean become more noticed, all of a sudden the two island fishermen will be approached by the sea creature, yet not as well as the two fishermen hopes. Next, their boat will become tossed to and fro, as the rippling effect on the ocean waters are about to turn into waves. The two fishermen believes, the *Yamaly* must be coming close to their boat; then as the second fishermen, with his almost too old camera, gets ready to capture some pictures of the sea creature; all of a sudden their near old boat, is tossing harder than before. Next, the other fisherman will handle his fishing spear, to get ready to take a hit at the Yamaly, such as if he can.

"Get ready *mon*, I believe the sea monster is near," the first fisherman says, although he is about to become a little frightened, instead of having proof that he and his friend has really seen the *Yamaly*.

"There it goes!" the second fisherman shouts, then as the top front of the sea creature plunges back down into the ocean waters, the plunge would be so strong, it would cause a wave almost ten feet up in the air, then it would cause the two fishermen's boat to almost crash just because of the wave.

"We have seen it again, let's get out of here *mon*; the *sea monster* is dangerous," the first fisherman would say, then suddenly their boat will have a feeling, as if it is being pulled by something, more stronger than the warm, island winds around the islands of the Bahamas. Yet, before either of the two fishermen can at least row their way back to the seashore, their boat will feel at the moment, as if it is being lifted by something, now the boat is sailing on the back of whatever very fast towards the seashore.

It would be after when the two fishermen's boat has finally landed on the seashore, the boat has a hole in it the size of a car's tire. The two fishermen do not want to find out any more about the *Yamaly*; next as the two now near frightened fisherman are running away from their almost sunken boat; the two can also hear the well-known wailing sound, which is all too familiar of the *Yamaly*. As the two fishermen keeps on running, the sea-dino is now on the far side of the island, watching with its two prehistoric eyes, at the fishermen who are running away. If the *Yamaly* can laugh such as humans can, the two fishermen would hear the sea creature doing the like.

Later, the *sea-dino* would plunge back down into the ocean waters around the islands of the Bahamas. As the two are trying to escape one of the fishermen has lost his camera, and the other one has lost his fishing spear. As both items are falling down deep into the ocean, the near old camera, which had belonged to one of the fishermen, seems to be strangely flashing with its old flash bulbs, as it sinks further and further down. Ever since the two fishermen's close encounter of the sea creature, known as the *Yamaly,* the two would never, ever again go out among the ocean waters around their islands of the Bahamas.

When a new morning arrives, Uncle Joel Ato will notice his own fishing boat, seems to be damaged. He knew why the item is the way it is, even though Uncle Joel Ato thinks now as he looks at his fishing boat, if his two relatives; Onandi and Sandi Bello had gone out to the ocean waters, to take a look see at the sea creature; it is probably the reason why his boat is almost damaged.

He would decide to forget about the damaged boat, and then later

Uncle Joel Ato while talking with Mr. Bello one early morning, Uncle Joel Ato would talk about his damaged boat. Mostly because of family, as well as out of island warmth Mr. Bello would go ahead to consent to buy Uncle Joel Ato a new boat. During the same day, Mr. Bello and Uncle Joel Ato will talk about the fairy tales also the sea creature, which both men believes is the reason why there are more visitors to the islands of the Bahamas.

Uncle Joel Ato, would not talk about his worries on just what may have happened to his boat; although Uncle Joel Ato will hear how Mr. Bello has already warned his two children not to go out to far in the ocean—just because. "Children can be too curious," is all Mr. Bello says, then after Uncle Joel Ato promises a much better catch, the two island relatives would be saying good-bye to each other; so Uncle Joel Ato can go out to go fishing for his family, as well as sell some of his catch in one of the local markets.

After setting up his fishing equipment, then readying up his boat, soon Uncle Joel Ato will be out sailing on the ocean waters, also again the winds are blowing a welcoming warmth of air. As his new boat, sails on the calm waters, Uncle Joel Ato as he waits for a catch, will utter a silent prayer to the old, sea spirit of the islands known as the *Yamalla*. Uncle

Joel Ato had not prayed to the ancient, yet not too true spirit, ever since he was only a boy; yet he feels at the time he must though. When only three hours of his fishing time has passed, Uncle Joel Ato will have more than enough fishes in his fishing basket; next he will notice something floating near his new boat, as Uncle Joel Ato rows closer and closer to the seashore.

After his boat is now close, and Uncle Joel Ato steps out of it, he will see an item, which looks like a camera. Even though it is almost sodden, it appears to Uncle Joel Ato as if the item can still work. When he is finished unloading his boat, then next taking home his catch of the day;

Uncle Joel Ato will go into the island city of the Bahamas, known as *Nassau* with the camera. After having the film exposed into black and white pictures, Uncle Joel Ato will tell the camera shopkeeper, it must be only a trick of the camera, then Uncle Joel Ato will go home; with more evidence perhaps a sea creature may exist somewhere around the ocean waters of the islands of the Bahamas.

Mostly because of the year round warm weather, three island twelve-year children, who are also best friends, will go out again to meet and greet a sea creature, known to the three as well as most of the other islanders, who believe; the *Yamaly*.

Since their fun and eventful day, Onandi and Sandi Bello, with Jearl Allen are from their day on of spending at the seashore, will forever want to see the sea creature. Neither of the three island twelve-year olds, has told their parents, about really seeing the Yamaly. All three knows, their parents would think the twelve-year olds are just *inventing* stories again, as usual, about the *Yamaly*.

When the three island friends, are now along the seashore; the three would also notice there are no other visitors at the seashore as well. Next, Onandi will retrieve the couch shell, which the three island twelve-year olds have been using, as a horn to signal out to the *Yamaly*. After three long sounds, from the couch shell, Onandi and Sandi, with Jearl will notice the same ripples of waves are starting to appear. The three will hold their young breaths, next Onandi, Sandi, and Jearl will see the top front of their sea creature, also known as their secret friend who lives in the ocean waters around their islands, slowly emerge up from the waters. They are all laughing with delight, as the *Yamaly*, slowly swims even closer to where all three of the island children are now standing.

Even though Sandi, Jearl, and Onandi are enjoying their time along the seashore, the three island twelve-year olds are also being cautious, as the sea creature is swimming closer and closer to the seashore. When the three are just far enough, at least to stay safe in spite of; Sandi, Jearl, and Onandi will just stare at the ancient, prehistoric *sea-dino*. As they keep watching, the *Yamaly*, will just lower its twenty-five feet body with most of it still in the ocean waters, as if it is signaling to the island children, it really implies no harm whatsoever.

"What is it, trying to do?" Jearl Allen is asking, and she can also see her father's face, if he were along the seashore with Jearl and her two friends, as they all are seeing the *Yamaly*, so close yet so far away.

"I don't know. Maybe we should have brought it some fishes," Sandi Bello is now saying, until her brother

Onandi notices another pail of fresh fish.

"Here is some, we can toss it out to it," Onandi is now saying, as he is getting the pail of fresh fishes, to get ready to toss out to the *Yamaly*.

"Where did those fishes come from?" asks Sandi, then next the three island, twelve-year olds are walking slowly towards the sea creature, as it keeps its twenty-five feet body still lying on the seashore, and the other part of its body, still reclined in the ocean waters. Of all the three island children, it would be Onandi who will take the first step in approaching the *Yamaly*. When Onandi Bello is just a few feet away from the sea creature, he would toss the fishes from the pail;

just close enough for the *Yamaly* to have another meal, from its three island friends.

Right now, Onandi will go back and stand near Sandi also Jearl, then the three twelve-year olds, will just sit and watch the Yamaly, the sea creature slowly eat and swallow down each fish, whole. Next, the twenty-five feet sea creature will lift up its top front; then turns around the rest of its lizard like body, to go back into the ocean waters. Also at the same time, Sandi, Onandi and Jearl are walking closer to the area along the seashore of where the *Yamaly* had been reclined; also, there is almost a hole from its lumbering body.

When the sea creature is just far enough out into the ocean waters, it would then leap up its twenty-five feet body; as if it is grateful for what Sandi, Onandi and Jearl had did for it. The three island children will laugh and jump up and down, as the Yamaly continues to leap while at the same time, causing a wave of at least six feet to go up against the children. After the three island friends, return home; Onandi and Sandi Bello, also Jearl Allen are drenched from the wave caused by the sea creature known to them all, *truthfully* to the twelve-year olds as the *Yamaly*. During the same night and before going to bed along with her family, Jearl Allen will hear her father talk about some pictures, which some fisherman had, showing the sea creature. Even though the fisherman is someone Mr. Allen knows, it is still not too sure, rather or not it is photos of the *Yamaly*.

CHAPTER 6

Before the seasons of when, most visitors are visiting the islands of the Bahamas, is about to end; the other remaining visitors, are again along the seashores of one certain area of the islands, to try and have one last glimpse of a well-known sea-dino known as the *Yamaly*. They are all there, almost ten of the visitors, with their cameras, and binoculars pointing out towards the ocean waters, which surrounds the certain islands, as the warm winds blow over the area; the palm trees are now swaying causing a crunching like sound, as the visitors sit and wait.

After almost three hours, of most of the visitors waiting for the *Yamaly*; when there is still no sighting of the sea-dino, some of them will start to pack up all of the items which the visitors had brought along, then walk away one by one—some of the visitors are now disappointed, just because. When they are now all gone away, the sun is now starting to set with the skies above showing a cool, shade of blue. As the warm, tropical winds blow, and if the visitors had just stayed longer — at least they all would have their chance to see a glimpse of the *sea-dino's* tail fin, as it swims farther back into the ocean waters, surrounding the certain area of the islands of the Bahamas.

When a new morning arrives, Uncle Joel Ato will go out for a walk, along the seashore, which is something he enjoys. As he walks along, Uncle Joel Ato can see some of the odds and ends the visitors has left behind, strolled along the seashore; some of it is mostly empty cans of soda with empty bags of what it seems to Uncle Joel Ato, probably snacks the visitors had brought with them. Even though the tourist season would be coming to a close, Uncle Joel Ato also knows, some of the island children would be out along the seashores of the island, to pick up the odds and ends of what the visitors has left behind; next the children would run along, and the seashore of the island would be clean as usual.

After Uncle Joel Ato, finds an old palm tree, which has fallen down mostly because of its old age, he would sit down and just think about the camera, which Uncle Joel Ato had found, and then later had the film in it developed. *"If the person or persons knew just how valuable the photos are, they would not have left the camera behind,*" Uncle Joel Ato is thinking, as he keeps his gaze out towards the wide, ocean waters. Uncle Joel Ato, also has a good feeling, his two cousins Onandi and Sandi Bello, may have seen the *Yamaly*.

Of the years he has told some of the stories, about the *sea-dino;* yet Uncle Joel Ato never had realized his two young cousins, would take the make-believe stories to heart; so much so; Sandi and Onandi Bello will go out along the seashore, with hopes of seeing the *Yamaly* one day. Uncle Joel Ato, although he really was not for sure; had believed his two relatives, may have taken out his near old boat one day; yet Uncle Joel Ato is grateful such as if Onandi and Sandi Bello did do likewise, they both returned safely, although later on Uncle Joel Ato was given a new one, by his two cousins parents.

As he sits on, Uncle Joel Ato will think of something rather good to do for his two cousins, Onandi and Sandi Bello, such as if the two really believe the sea-dino actually exits. While he thinks on, all of a sudden, Uncle Joel Ato as he still sits on the old, fallen down palm tree, will see something far out into the ocean waters. Right now, he will stand up from the palm tree, and walk very slowly and more closely to the edge of the seashore, to have an even more look-see. Of all the years of Uncle Joel Ato, from the days of him when he was, a child too; had thought he would never, ever again see the *Yamaly*. Uncle Joel Ato, knew most sea creatures if they do exist, no one really knows just how long would the ancient animals live on earth— even up to this very day.

When Uncle Joel Ato, is just close enough to the edge of the seashore, his very, near aging eyes would behold the sea dino known as the Yamaly. From the distance of where he is standing, Uncle Joel Ato can see very clearly also the top front of the Yamaly, then as the *sea-dino* swims on; Uncle Joel Ato can really see one side of the sea-dino, as well as one of its huge fins. As the Yamaly swims on and on, next it would emerge its twenty-five feet long body, back down into the ocean waters, even though still Uncle Joel Ato can see only a blur like image of the *sea-dino;* then next it will be gone completely. When Uncle Joel Ato, turns around to walk home, the same ripples from the ocean, can now be seen; next, the sun will start to set again.

During the same evening, Uncle Joel Ato will first begin to write to his two cousins, Onandi and Sandi Bello. He will explain to both of them in writing, how even when Uncle Joel Ato was just a small boy, he too had believed in the *Yamaly*. Uncle Joel Ato, would even explain in the writings to the two cousins, when he was only a boy as well, Uncle Joel Ato had believed, the *sea-dino* could only be seen, when the *Yamalla*, a so-named, ancient god of the seas would call upon the *Yamaly*.

When he is finished writing, Uncle Joel Ato will place the five pieces of paper, along with the photos of the sea-dino, which had developed while being in *Nassau* in an envelope. Then he would seal the eight by eleven, light brown envelope; then next Uncle Joel Ato will think of the right time, when he would present the envelope to his two cousins; Onandi and Sandi Bello. Matter of what he has just did for his two relative, Uncle Joel Ato hopes, when the two has the envelope, both Sandi and Onandi

Bello, would have out grown the make-believe stories of the *Yamaly*— although Uncle Joel Ato has placed some photos, with his letters to his two relatives which could prove to be just the opposite.

When Mr. Allen returns home from work, he will see again, his only daughter Jearl is out, perhaps along the seashore playing with her two best friends. Although Mr. Allen is glad, the season for the visitors will be soon over; he is now thinking about his daughter Jearl, and her questions about the *Yamaly*. Mr. Allen has too, been thinking about the time when his wife, and their daughter Jearl, were asked by some visitors about the

Yamaly. Mr. Allen is very much proud, his wife had told him about the way their daughter Jearl, had answered the question; mostly because Mr. Allen still thinks the fairy tales about the sea-dino, is really *hog-ocean wash.*

Mr. Allen though, has respect for his own islands culture, although he believes some of it all, can be taken almost a little far out. Except some of the ideas, such as if a so named *sea-dino*, really exists, and then the sea creature must be one, which has not become all the way extinct. Since his own school days, above all when he was the alike age as his daughter Jearl; Mr. Allen had been taught about prehistoric animals, such as the

Yamaly; yet the giant lizards are all suppose to be very much no longer.

After seeing his daughter Jearl is not home, and his wife is working in another place in their home; Mr. Allen will just walk outside, and sit on the wooden porch of the Allen home. As he sits, and looks out even across the sandy seashores, all the way out to the wide ocean waters, Mr. Allen will begin to think, if by chance such a prehistoric, *sea-dino* could be somewhere swimming in the ocean waters around the islands of the Bahamas.

Next, he would dismiss the notion out of his mind; yet before Mr. Allen takes one step back inside of the home, he shares with his wife and only daughter, Mr. Allen eyes would be seeing in the far out of the ocean waters, something which looks to be the top front, of an sea animal, although what Mr. Allen is seeing, is not a *dolphin* and really not a *whale*. All of sudden, what Mr. Allen is actually seeing, will emerge back down into the ocean waters, as quickly as it had appeared. *"Hog-ocean wash,"* Mr. Allen is thinking, although he still is thinking about just what was out there in the ocean waters, Mr. Allen will remind him to talk to Jearl, to be very, very careful while she enjoys her moments of playtime along the seashore.

Even if a certain group of reptiles had lived on the earth so many millions perhaps billions of years earlier, the terrible lizards would soon be no longer roaming on the earth, until finally the dinosaurs would become extinct. Later, after the ending of a specific time, all of the so-called dinosaurs had died out. Some persons, who usually studies at times about pre-historic dinosaurs, would have another idea. When after the change in the earth's climate, at the time, the giant lizards had begun to eat one another, maybe to live—yet, some other experts believed a huge meteor hit the earth, then the giant lizards would be no longer.

Except for one so-named, giant lizard, who some other persons believed, also the people of one of the islands of the Bahamas, thinks in their own ocean waters; there could one such *giant* lizard. Besides, there have been only small reports about seeing an animal, with a giant top front, and fins along its side, much like other sea animals. As well, the so named sea creature, is *jumbo* than most of the other sea life, which exists today. Then again, from the reports of the very few people, who may have seen the well-known *Yamaly;* they all say it looks like the dinosaurs of long ago, except the certain *sea-dino* has fins, and it just lives out into the ocean waters.

Even if all other reports and sightings are true, not even the *Yamaly* knows how long it would be swimming around the ocean waters, of a certain island in the Bahamas. Just as most of its prehistoric beings before it, the Yamaly just may become no longer, perhaps because of time. Until then, three island children, will continue their own time of seeing the *sea-dino*, much to their own parents dismay. Sandi and Onandi Bello, with their friend Jearl Allen, all believe the *Yamaly*, will live on and on, such as if the *sea-dino* can remain to swim here and there in its own area, of ocean waters, around the island. As well, with the ending of the tourist season, the three island children can go out along the seashore to meet and greet their new *sea-dino*, at least until they perhaps can no longer see it.

CHAPTER 7

During a cool evening of the day, of the Allen household, and while sitting down with her own family, Jearl Allen will hear that her two parents are somewhat grateful, the tourist season is now over. Even if some of the visitors to the islands of the Bahamas, had came along, to really view a well known, *sea-dino* known as the Yamaly; a certain island of the

Bahamas, where the sea creature can usually seen; has earned sums of money just because.

When their evening meal is now over, the Allen family would go outside to sit on their wide wooden porch, and just talk, another moment Jearl has always enjoyed with her family. During the same night, there is a new, full moon, casting its glow all over the ocean waters, which can be seen just a distance away from the Allen home. As Jearl's parents are sitting close to each other, while Jearl is sitting on one of the steps of the wooden porch, next it would be Jearl's father; Mr. Allen who will begin to talk about the *sea-dino*, known all around the islands of the Bahamas; as the *Yamaly*.

"Of all the years, especially when I was your age Jearl, I never did see the *Yamaly*," Mr. Allen is now saying, to his only daughter, as Jearl is looking out towards the ocean waters.

"Don't tell me, you really did not believe it really existed," Mrs. Allen says, while using the past tense of the sea creature.

"Some of the island folks, during my younger years, had claimed to have seen it. Well, I remembered one certain fisherman, had claimed he almost caught the Yamaly," Mr. Allen says, also Jearl has turned around just slightly, to hear more of what her beloved father, has said about the *sea-dino*, mainly about a fisherman some years ago, who had almost caught the prehistoric sea creature.

"I do believe, because of what the fisherman had told, started all of this *babble* about the sea creature", Mrs. Allen says.

"Do you believe, the *Yamaly* is out there somewhere in our ocean waters Jearl?" her father Mr. Allen has now asked, also now Jearl is looking out across at the ocean waters.

"I have not seen it, I do hope it is for real," Jearl Allen says, and she hopes too; her parents cannot be aware of if their only daughter could be telling fibs about the sea creature.

Ever since Jearl, and her other two friends Sandi also Onandi Bello, has been playing around the seashore, then by a move of luck, had seen the *Yamaly;* the three best island friends, has really decided to keep the secret of actually being so close to the *Yamaly*, all three could have touched the *sea-dino*. While the Allen family, keeps on sitting outside enjoying their family evening together; the full moon over the certain area of the islands of the Bahamas, appears to be rising up higher over the night sky.

Next, before all three of the Allen family walk back inside of their own home, all of a sudden Jearl Allen will hear the distant, yet whale like sound of the *Yamaly*. Jearl Allen will stop, before she walks back inside of the house, then it would be her mother who will ask Jearl, if something is wrong.

"We must get back inside, it's getting late," Mrs. Allen says, in her pleasant, island accent.

"Did you hear that?" Jearl asks, with a delight in her young voice, which is about to confuse her mother, even though Mr. Allen has walked back inside of their home.

"Only the waves my child, now come on inside of the house Jearl," Mrs. Allen says, yet Jearl will keep standing, then next she will walk off the wide, wooden front porch of the Allen home; all because Jearl Allen can hear the whale like sounds of the *sea-dino*, just a distant away from the Allen house.

"Come inside Jearl", is all Mrs. Allen says, next Jearl will walk back inside, as the whale sounds of the sea-dino are starting to fade. What is so usual about the Allen family's evening, it seems as if Jearl's two parents may have not heard the sea creature. While she is in her own bedroom, trying to fall asleep in her soft, snug bed, Jearl Allen can still hear the fading, yet distant sounds of the *Yamaly*, until the sea-dino can no longer be heard throughout the full, moonlit night.

The next early morning hours, Uncle Joel Ato would go out again to begin his work to catch fish. The sun as usual, is casting its warm yet golden rays upon the ocean waters; also, Uncle Joel Ato has other reasons for feeling so good. Although he had given his two cousins, Sandi and Onandi Bello, a gift of a letter along with some photographs of what could have been the Yamaly; Uncle Joel Ato is gladder there are no more visitors out along the seashore line, of the island where he lives with his family. Also Uncle Joel Ato, can go fishing without being disturbed by some onlookers who only wants to have a view, of an well-known sea monster, which it would seem had lived some millions of years earlier.

Even if Uncle Joel Ato is no person who knows so much about prehistoric dinosaurs, at times it seems the old islander, cannot believe such a giant lizard, which lives out in the ocean waters surrounding the islands, still exists. After he places all of his fishing gear inside of his new fishing boat, the winds are now starting to blow, and the warm air is not blowing so fiercely, which would have Uncle Joel Ato to begin his fishing for the day.

As he sails further out towards the ocean, yet not to far Uncle Joel Ato when he is just so far out to begin his fishing, Uncle Joel Ato will stop the rowing of his new boat, then cast one of his fishing nets outside of the boat. While he sits and waits, Uncle Joel Ato will start to whistle, then all of a sudden, the near old islander will feel something perhaps at the bottom of his boat. Although Uncle Joel Ato is not afraid, yet for the certain fishing day, he does not plan to be tossed out of his own fishing boat. Uncle Joel Ato, is expecting a good catch, all became of the income he needs for his family, as well for everyone to eat the seafood.

As he boats continues to toss, after a few minutes, Uncle Joel Ato will not feel the boat rock, until his near aging eyes happens to look closer down at the ocean waters. The near old islander, can see the ripples are appearing again, which has become somewhat of a sign, for some of the other islanders, whenever the *Yamaly* do an appearance, either near or faraway from the seashores. Right now, Uncle Joel Ato will keep still in his boat, all of sudden the well-known *sea-dino* can be seen almost a few yards away, from the very area where Uncle Joel Ato is now fishing.

"There you are. Been expecting you, since there was a full moon last night," Uncle Joel Ato is now saying, in his full island accent, also as if the sea creature can understand most of the words, the near aging islander is saying. With its top front showing, the *Yamaly* can actually be seen clearly now, next Uncle Joel Ato will notice his net is also full of the catch of the day. After he lifts up the fishing net, and as the fishes inside of it, flip around; next Uncle Joel Ato, will gather up five of the largest of his catch.

Now, he will toss out the five, large fish which are the size of a salmon; then as Uncle Joel Ato keeps looking at the sea creature, gathering up the seafood into its mouth, which is rather long; next when the *Yamaly* seems to be full of the catch of the day; the *sea-dino* will turn around its twenty-five foot long body, swim its way back farther out into the ocean waters. When the sea-dino has swam away, Uncle Joel Ato will row his new boat back towards the seashore, so he can rest before he go out and sells some of his catch.

As he gather up all of fishes he had caught, then place them in two larger baskets with lids, Uncle Joel Ato is thinking perhaps he should had his two cousins, Sandi and Onandi to come along with him. Uncle Joel Ato again thinks it would not have been wise, all because of the appearance of the *sea-dino* known as the *Yamaly*. After he places the two large baskets, holding his catch of the day, on a wagon which Uncle Joel Ato has been having, ever since he was a young boy; the near old island fisherman; begins to think just how long would the *Yamaly* live-in in view of how old the *sea-dino* is suppose to be.

"Probably the Yamaly will not live as long as me", Uncle Joel Ato is now thinking, as he is walking on home with his catch of the day. Then

again, although Uncle Joel Ato has a good reason to believe what he is now believing, no one really knows how old the *sea-dino* is; except if one counts millions and millions of years, also Uncle Joel Ato is not even close to being the same years as the *sea-dino*.

"Don't go too near the ocean Jearl," Mrs. Allen is saying to her only daughter, as Jearl is walking out to meet with her two island friends for a day of fun—and perhaps to see the *Yamaly* again. She has one idea of why she is starting to feel about, a secret which Jearl and her two other friends, Sandi and Onandi Bello are keeping to them. The three island children, have actually seen the *Yamaly*, a *sea-dino* which is about to become absent.

Jearl Allen believes her father, when he had told her; there have been no other prehistoric giant lizards on the face of planet earth, for millions and millions of years. Then again, Jearl Allen has found it rather hard to believe, some meteor from the sky, which her father had explained to her; could have killed off the giant lizards. Jearl Allen has one book, which she owns, have pictures of the prehistoric, giant lizards; and some of the words Jearl cannot hardy say; no matter how fascinating the pictures in her book about dinosaurs looks.

Even while attending school on the island, Jearl Allen did not study too much about the prehistoric animals. At times though, it would still add to her curiosity about the prehistoric, giant lizards, which could had roamed from one area of the earth to another one; at least until the giant lizards all died out. Now, as she is walking closer to the seashore, Jearl Allen can see her two best friends, are already there waiting for Jearl.

"Hey, has it come out again?" Jearl is asking, and she can see Onandi has his couch shell, which he has been using, to signal out to the *sea-dino*.

"Not yet. My brother and I, would like to show you what I uncle, has given us," Sandy Bello is saying, as she walks closer to Jearl to show her best friend, a book with photographs of perhaps the *sea-dino* the *Yamaly*.

"Wow! Where did you get this?" Jearl Allen is asking her lovely, brown eyes are open wide, as she looks at some photographs of the sea-dino, very much close up.

"Our Uncle Joel Ato, he though, does not believe the photographs are real," Sandi Bello is now saying, and then Jearl will ask how her two best friend's uncle did, was able to take the photographs.

"He only told us, he found the camera along the seashore. Then he took the camera to *Nassau*", Onandi says, as he keeps his eyes looking out towards the ocean.

"The photographs look real enough", is all Jearl Allen says, also as she and Sandi Bello keeps looking at the book with the photos of the *Yamaly* in it; all of sudden Onandi will blow into his conch shell. Right now, Jearl and Sandi are no longer looking in the book; next Onandi will blow even harder into the conch shell. As the three island friends wait, it seems as if the *Yamaly* may not have heard its *signal*.

"Try again Onandi," his sister Sandi is saying, then all of a sudden; the three island twelve-year olds, will see the same ripples of the ocean waters start to happen.

"He has heard us!" shouts Jearl, then as the ripples become more so, next the three island children, will see the top front of the Yamaly; even though it is a distance away from the seashore, where Jearl, Sandi and Onandi are now standing.

"Where are the fishes?" Jearl ask, next Sandi will tell her, they have forgotten about the seafood. As the three island children, keep their gazes upon the *Yamaly*—it seems as if the sea-dino is starting to do back flips, way out into the ocean waters. The back flips of the *sea-dino* are happening so fast, there would be waves of almost six feet tall coming up on the seashores, where the three twelve-year olds are still standing.

"It must see us," Sandi now says, and then next the three island

143

children will shout, and wave their arms about as if they are all trying to get the attention of the *sea-dino*.

"I have an idea," Jearl says, as she talks on to her two best friends, Jearl Allen will suggest they all should have enough fishes for the *sea-dino*.

"Let' try to get at least two pails full, if we can," Sandi says, and then after all three will say yes just because, next they all will keep their gazes out towards the ocean waters. Now, the *sea-dino* is swimming farther and farther out to sea; until Jearl, Sandi, and her brother Onandi, can only see a faint glimpse of the *Yamaly's* prehistoric tail and fins, along the sides of its giant body.

During the very same night, of the same day, Onandi would have a harder time of trying to fall asleep. He along with his sister Sandi had heard their Uncle Joel Ato talk to their Onandi and Sandi parents, about his fishing. Onandi can notice as he listened, his Uncle Joel Ato had also earned more money for his fishing catch, by selling some of the seafood at the local market. Later that night, when Onandi's parents were asleep, and his Uncle Joel Ato had gone off to home, both twelve-year old island children had gathered up enough fish, for to them, the two island children's sea-dino friend known as the *Yamaly*.

A while later, the two island children will go to their bedrooms to sleep, at least for a while; then Onandi will find him unable to sleep. After he gets up from his bed, Onandi will see his sister is still asleep then he will walk to a desk their father had built, for Onandi and his sister Sandi. When he sees there is paper, and a pen lying on the desk; Onandi will sit down at the desk to begin to write a poem, about the *Yamaly*, which has been going around and around in Onandi Bello's twelve-year old brain. Next, Onandi will start to write the words on paper, in honor of his sea-dino friend, the *Yamaly*.

Once upon a time,
There lived a sea creature
Who lived in the sea.

The Yamaly is real, except no one
would agree, just as real the
Yamaly can be.
At night, when the moon is full
The Yamaly would swim up to
the seashore, until it swims away, and
then the Yamaly would be seen no
more.

After reading his poem, the way it is written, almost brings tears to Onandi Bello's eyes. Next, he will place his poem away, tucked inside one of the drawers of the desk, yet before he finally goes to sleep; Onandi believes he can hear the whale like sounds, coming from the ocean waters. He will walk to the window, in Onandi and Bello's bedroom also as he peers out more so; Onandi believes he has seen the *Yamaly*, out swimming in the ocean waters. As well, there is another full moon out, and rays from it are glistening on the ocean waters, just as Uncle Joel Ato has always told his two young cousins just because.

When a new day arrives, Jearl and her two other best friends, Onandi and Sandi Bello, would once again go out to the seashore, to catch another look-see at the Yamaly. The three island children though, had decided not to go out in another boat, since Onandi and Sandi Bello's uncle had almost griped about his last boat, which was almost broken apart. The three island twelve-year olds, are also grateful Uncle Joel Ato perhaps has not one idea, if it was Jearl, Sandi and Onandi who would had taken the boat out to the ocean waters, to find the sea-dino.

With the two pails of fishes, and Onandi Bello holding his couch shell, all three of the island children, will decide to go just a ways farther than usual. Except this moment, Jearl, Sandi, and Onandi will walk down farther along the seashore, to try and get a better look-see at the Yamaly. When all three have walked just farther too almost to the other side of the island, Sandi, Jearl and Onandi would place all of the items down which they had brought; then next

Onandi Bello will lift the couch up to his lips, then blow into the seashell just as hard as his twelve-year old lungs can muster.

As the warm, island winds began to blow softly, swaying some of the palm trees, which are dotted along the seashore, where Jearl, Sandi, and Onandi are now standing; all of a sudden, the same ripples, which the three island twelve-year olds can notice, are now happening, as all three of them wait. As the ripples become more in plain sight, next the three island children can already see the sea-dino, just some yards away from where Sandi, Jearl, and Onandi are standing.

"It looks as if the Yamaly is just close enough," Jearl Allen will now say, as the sea-dino appears to be just swimming in the ocean waters, yet from still such a faraway distance.

"Blow again into the conch Onandi," his sister Sandi is now saying, then as Onandi gets ready to blow much harder into the conch seashell, right now the sea-dino is starting to swim closer and close to the seashore, of where the three island twelve-year olds are still standing.

"It's swimming closer!" Jearl is now shouting, all of sudden, the three island twelve-year olds, can see the Yamaly, very close up. As they all hold their young breaths, the sea-dino will swim very slowly, towards the young humans, who are along the seashore; also Jearl, Sandi and Onandi will just step back further, as the sea-dino, with its giant, lizard like body, swims slower and slower to the seashore, until only its top front, and its long, thick can be seen by the three island children.

Even though Jearl, Sandi and Onandi have been told to not venture to close to the seashore, what the three twelve-year olds will see with their own, young curious eyes, will be an event, all three just may hold in their own hearts—for the rest of their own lives. Right now, the Yamaly will lower the top front as if it is trying to rest; also, the ocean waters are washing back and forth on its body, even now, Jearl, Sandi, and Onandi can see a slight look-see at one of its fins.

"Should we walk closer to it?" Jearl is now asking, as the sea-dino keeps half of its prehistoric body, close to the seashore, its eyes appearing as if they are slowly closing shut.

"Very carefully, we really don't know how dangerous the Yamaly is", Onandi says, as he lifts up one of the pails of fishes, to feed to the sea-dino.

"You first," his sister Sandi says, as she is now standing some feet away from the sea-dino, also Sandi is not as close to the Yamaly, as her brother and friend Jearl are.

"I will go with you Onandi," Jearl says, and right now, she is not at all afraid, as before. Jearl Allen cannot believe, right along the same seashore, of where she and her other two friends live; there is a sea-dino which has been known as some sort of island legend, is laying as if it is resting, on one of the islands of the Bahamas.

Now, Onandi and Jearl are walking very carefully as well as to get closer to the Yamaly; and they can hear some heavy breathing coming from the sea-dino; and its almost huge, prehistoric eyes are appearing as if they are closing shut. Onandi is now even closer to the Yamaly, then next as he places down one of the pails of fishes; Onandi as his sister, holds her breath just because, will reach out his twelve-year old right hand, and pat the Yamaly just carefully on the top front of its body.

"There now Yamaly, we won't hurt you; we are your friends," Onandi only says, yet the sea-dino will just lie still, as its breaths are about to become more thin. Right now, Jearl has walked just as close to the Yamaly, as Onandi have; and she too will bend down closer, so she can pat the sea-dino on the top front as well.

"I hope it's now dying," Jearl will say, and she sounds as if she is going to cry.

"Maybe it's hungry. We have not seen the Yamaly, for days now; and we have not brought it fishes to eat for awhile," Onandi says, also at the same moment his sister Sandi has walked closer to the sea-dino; yet she will not pat the Yamaly on the top front, just because.

"Let' feed it, who will go first?" Sandi has now asked, then next her very brave brother, will be the first to try and place at least one of the fishes in the pail, inside of the *Yamaly's* prehistoric mouth. As the three twelve-year olds remain still, as Onandi takes one of the fishes, then as he places it closer to the *Yamaly's* mouth; the sea-dino will open it very slowly, showing only very small teeth, which seems to be from the front to the very back of its giant mouth.

"Wow!' all three will exclaim, as the Yamaly eats one fish at a time, as Onandi places them in its mouth. Next, it would what the sea-dino would do, which will almost startle the three twelve-year olds. The *Yamaly* will all of sudden, lift ups its giant top front; causing Sandi, Onandi and Jearl to run farther from it. The sea-dino would now look at the young humans, along the seashore; then it would turn around its twenty-five feet body, to swim back into the ocean waters.

Now, the sea-dino will swim at a much faster speed, as it goes farther out into the ocean waters, until it's just far enough; then next Onandi, along with Sandi also Jearl; will begin to toss the two pails of fishes, until all of the seafood is gone—as well as eaten up by the *Yamaly*. Next, for almost the remainder of the day, the three island children will just sit and watch the sea-dino, as it tosses up and down into the ocean waters; causing waves of only five feet high, along the seashore.

Before the sun sets, and the three island children get ready to go home; they all will promise among each other, not to tell not even their own parents, about the good day all of them had. While carrying back the two empty pails, and Onandi carrying his conch shell in one of his arms, the three island children will talk about just what would become of their sea-dino friend, when all of them are soon all grown up. It would be Jearl Allen who both Onandi and Sandi they would just have to wait until the time present itself then. Until, the three island twelve-year olds, will just every so often, venture far along the seashore to catch a glimpse of the Yamaly, as well as to feed it.

The three twelve-year olds, are unaware of just how long most prehistoric sea animals, such as the Yamaly actually lives. Even as long as the moon lit nights continue, along the sandy seashores of the islands of the Bahamas, one just may can catch a glimpse of the Yamaly; yet until then only three island children, who are best friends will only have the chance to see the sea-dino, of course.

During the same night, Jearl Allen can hardly fall asleep, just because of what she has seen, as well as did with her two best island friends. As well, before Jearl falls to sleep, she will take down her one book about dinosaurs, and read it again, while looking over all of the artsy pictures of the giant lizards, which supposedly had roamed the earth, until some meteor or the changes in the climate, had the giant lizards to become extinct.

Before Jearl closes the book, she will notice the light of full moon, is casting through the curtains in her bedroom. After she places the book back, which has the pictures and stories about dinosaurs away; Jearl will walk to her bedroom window, and then take a pause. As she stands near the bedroom window, Jearl Allen at the moment thinks she can hear the whale like sounds of the Yamaly. As she stands there to keep hearing, Jearl will become sleepy; yet as soon as she is now in bed; the sea-dino's top front can be seen, its shadow being casted on the ocean waters, as it swims its way back farther out into the ocean.

Onandi and Sandi Bello will just sit outside on their front porches, and talk among each other about what they had did with their friend Jearl. As well on the same night, their Uncle Joel Ato did not come over, as he usually does, most with his fresh catch of fishes. Onandi and Sandi Bello are also hoping their Uncle Joel Ato would not notice; if some of his catch of a certain day; had been thrown out to a prehistoric, sea-dino which Sandi and Onandi Bello, thinks their uncle may not believe exists.

The same night, before both Sandi and Onandi fall asleep, Onandi will take out the photo book, which their Uncle Joel Ato had put together for his two cousins. As Onandi sit and read the letters, also look at the photos, which their uncle had developed in *Nassau*, Onandi Bello is now thinking, as long as he lives; he has no *wish* to move away from his home, in the Bahamas. Just because of what he, his sister Sandi, and their best friend Jearl had an incident of seeing the Yamaly, then next patting the sea-dino as if it was some huge *sea puppy*; Onandi thinks as long as he lives on the islands, the Yamaly could be seen perhaps—*forever*. Next, before he places away the photo book, which his Uncle Joel Ato had given to Onandi and his sister Sandi; all of a sudden, Onandi believes right now; he can hear the whale like sounds of the Yamaly. Next, he will walk over to the window of the bedroom; all of sudden Onandi can hear the sounds yet faintly. As well, Onandi can see there is a full moon out tonight, also as he stands at the bedroom window; Onandi can see far away, the faint shadow of the sea-dino, perhaps swimming farther out into the ocean waters. Yes indeed, Onandi will stay as long as the island twelve-year so wishes, on a certain island of the Bahamas, which is where Onandi lives, all because of the Yamaly.

Uncle Joel Ato though, for the remainder of his days, would continue to go out and catch fish as usual. He had already seen the Yamaly countless of times, even though he believes his two cousins perhaps has seen the sea-dino, even more so. Uncle Joel Ato, also had some idea of perhaps why his old boat was almost broken in half; yet the near old island fisherman; would not scold at his two cousins even his worries were correct.

Then again, Uncle Joel Ato knew the sea-dino known as the *Yamaly*, with all of its ancient stories, could be what makes being a young child so much fun. Although Uncle Joel Ato, had been told make-believe stories about the *Yamaly*, to Uncle Joel Ato then; it all seemed as if the sea-dino is really real—even though the near, old island fisherman had only a few encounters with the sea-dino.

At times though, also especially when the islands of the Bahamas were teeming with visitors, Uncle Joel Ato had wondered if the sea-dino would be discovered—yet it has not. Uncle Joel Ato, hated to think just what would happen to the sea-dino if someone who is not a native of his own island, could do to the sea-dino, which has been seen mostly as a giant sea lizard, which could only be seen during a full moonlit night.

When a new morning arrives, Uncle Joel Ato will prepare to go out among the ocean waters to catch fish, and the sun is warm yet it is also being covered by billows of fluffy white clouds. After he sets his fishing gear into his new boat, Uncle Joel Ato will climb into his boat, then row slowly out just far enough out to the ocean waters so he can begin. When he is just far enough, Uncle Joel Ato will now cast out one of his nets and wait; then he too will hear the whale like sound, which is all too familiar to the near old island fisherman. Uncle Joel

Ato is thinking; he too just may share some of his catch of fishes, with a so named sea-dino, which is still known as some kind of legend. As well to Uncle Joel Ato, the Yamaly, is about to become just as famous as its other prehistoric relative, who may live in another part of the world, known as the *Loch Ness* sea monster.

Coming to a seashore near you!

The author Amina Harrison has written dozens of self-published novels, presently Miss Harrison at times writes fictional stories, geared towards the immediate school-aged children. In addition to her new children's novel; YAMALY, THE SEA-DINO, Miss Amina Harrison has written two other children's novels of the immediate ages for children; THE EGYPT GAME, and THE MAGIC ABC'S CEREAL. All available on amazon.com, in paperback as well as e-book formats.